S0-BFA-398

MAY THE
FORCE
BE WITH YOU

A GOLDEN BOOK • NEW YORK
Golden Books Publishing Company, Inc., Racine, Wisconsin 53404

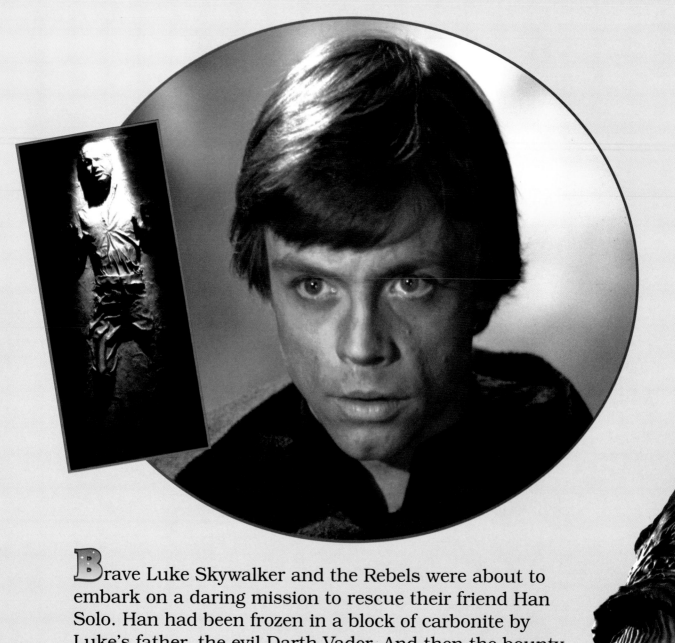

Brave Luke Skywalker and the Rebels were about to embark on a daring mission to rescue their friend Han Solo. Han had been frozen in a block of carbonite by Luke's father, the evil Darth Vader. And then the bounty hunter, Boba Fett, had handed Solo over to Jabba the Hutt, a sluglike crime lord.

As part of the rescue plan, Han's friend Lando Calrissian had disguised himself as a guard and sneaked into Jabba's palace. And Luke had sent his droids, C-3PO and R2-D2, ahead to prepare for his own arrival. But Jabba took the droids prisoner and forced them to work for him.

Soon afterward, a mysterious bounty hunter appeared at the palace with a prisoner—Han Solo's copilot, Chewbacca the Wookiee. The hunter demanded a reward for the capture of Chewbacca, and—

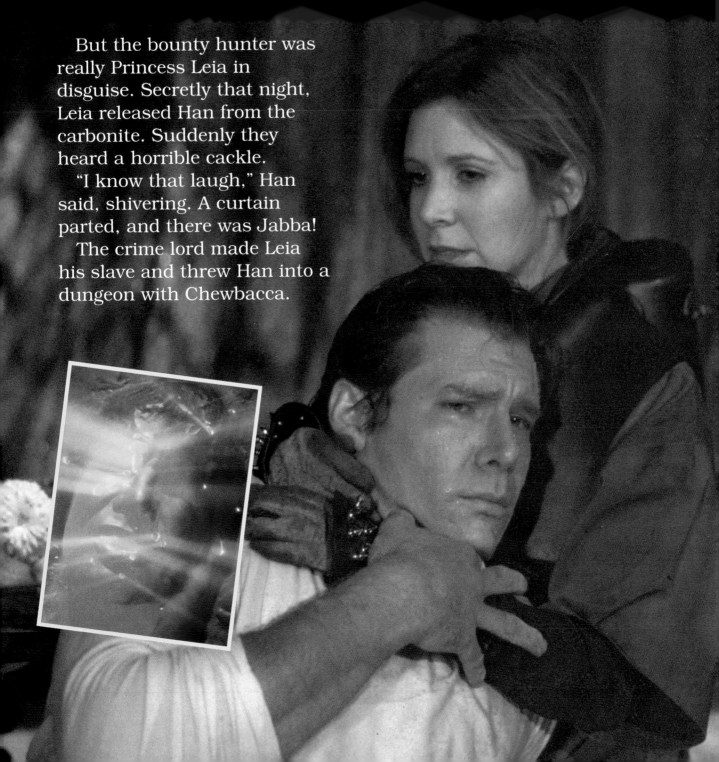

But the bounty hunter was really Princess Leia in disguise. Secretly that night, Leia released Han from the carbonite. Suddenly they heard a horrible cackle.

"I know that laugh," Han said, shivering. A curtain parted, and there was Jabba!

The crime lord made Leia his slave and threw Han into a dungeon with Chewbacca.

Just when things looked hopeless, Luke Skywalker arrived. He entered the palace, using a Jedi mind trick, and ordered the crime lord to release his friends.

Jabba laughed. "I will enjoy watching you die," he sneered.

Then the gangster hit a button that released a trapdoor under Luke's feet.

Luke dropped into a cell with a horrible monster called a rancor. Jabba watched happily as Luke fought off the vicious beast. After a terrible struggle, young Skywalker finally hit a switch that sent a massive iron door dropping down on the rancor. Jabba's nasty pet was crushed!

Jabba was furious! He took Luke, Han, and Chewbacca into the desert to face another monster—the terrible Sarlacc. The Sarlacc lived in a gaping pit and ate anything that fell into its gigantic mouth.

"Free us or die," Luke warned Jabba.

The crime lord only laughed and gave the order for Skywalker to be thrown into the Sarlacc pit.

On Jabba's sail barge, R2-D2 waited for Luke's signal—and then tossed the young Jedi his lightsaber! With help from Lando, Luke freed his friends and fought off Jabba's men. Soon the crime lord was defeated, and the heroes raced away in a desert skiff.

While Han, Leia, and the others returned to the Rebel fleet, Luke and R2-D2 went to see the Jedi Master, Yoda.

"No more training do you require," Yoda told Luke. "You must confront Darth Vader—then a Jedi you will be."

Yoda was very old and weak and told Luke that he would soon die. But before he passed away, he informed his young pupil that there was another Skywalker. Luke wondered who it could be.

Luke's question was answered by his old friend Obi-Wan Kenobi, who appeared before him. "You have a twin sister," Obi-Wan said. "You were both hidden at birth to protect you from the Emperor."

"Leia!" Luke said, realizing the truth. "Leia's my sister!"

Luke returned to the Rebel fleet, where he found the freedom fighters planning an attack on a new Imperial Death Star. Though still not completed, the gigantic battle station was protected by an energy shield powered by a generator on the forest moon of Endor.

The Rebel attack plan was simple: Han, Luke, Leia, Chewbacca, and the droids would disable the shield while Lando Calrissian would lead the fighter attack against the Death Star.

After landing on Endor, Han and the small band of Rebels met Wicket and the Ewoks, who brought the Rebels back to their tree-house village.

C-3PO could speak the Ewoks' language. He told them all about the war against the Empire, and the heroic adventures of Luke, Han, Leia, and the other freedom fighters. Since the Ewoks were also enemies of the evil Empire, they agreed to help destroy the energy shield.

But Darth Vader had his own mission. He had been searching the galaxy for his son Luke and was determined to make him join the Empire.

Luke could feel his father's presence on Endor and knew that he must go face him. So he surrendered to Vader, hoping to turn him away from the dark side of the Force.

"I know there is good in you," Luke told his father.

"It is too late for me, Son," said Vader. "The Emperor will show you the true nature of the Force."

Vader took Luke to the Death Star to see the Emperor.

"Your friends on the Endor moon are walking into a trap, as is your Rebel fleet," the Emperor told Skywalker.

Feeling helpless, Luke struggled to control his rage.

"Take your lightsaber," the Emperor said to Luke. "Give in to your anger."

Luke seized his lightsaber and swung at the Emperor, but Darth Vader blocked Luke's blow—and father and son dueled again!

Meanwhile on Endor, Han led the attack on the energy-shield generator. But just as the Emperor had foretold, the generator bunker held a trap. Han, Leia, and Chewbacca were captured by an army of stormtroopers!

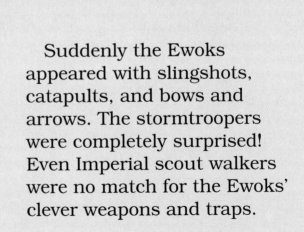

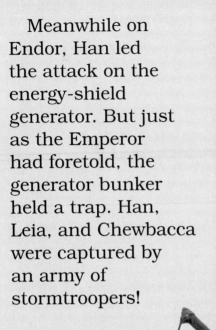

Suddenly the Ewoks appeared with slingshots, catapults, and bows and arrows. The stormtroopers were completely surprised! Even Imperial scout walkers were no match for the Ewoks' clever weapons and traps.

Back on the Death Star, Luke threw down his lightsaber.
"I'll never turn to the dark side," he said.

"Then you will be destroyed," the Emperor hissed. Powerful
lightning bolts flew from his hands and struck Luke.

But Darth Vader came to Luke's rescue. The once-evil lord
grabbed the Emperor and threw him down a bottomless shaft!

Vader was badly wounded by the Emperor.

"Luke, help me take this mask off," Vader said. For the first time, Luke looked upon the face of his father, Anakin Skywalker. As he lay dying, Anakin thanked Luke for having saved him from the dark side.

Carrying his father, Luke climbed into an Imperial shuttle and sped away.

With the energy shield destroyed, the Rebel pilots were able to attack the Death Star.

"All fighters follow me!" Lando cried. He piloted the *Millennium Falcon* into the battle station's main reactor shaft. With TIE fighters chasing him, Lando and the Rebels fired their cannons and sped out of the space station.

The Death Star blew up in a huge fireball!

The explosion was seen by the Rebels on Endor. They let out a great cheer. The evil Galactic Empire had been defeated!

That night, the Rebels celebrated in the Ewok village. Han, Leia, Chewbacca, Lando, C-3PO, R2-D2, and Luke were all happily reunited by a glowing bonfire.

At last, Luke Skywalker had become a Jedi Knight. Sneaking away from the noisy celebration, Luke saw three shining figures appear before him—Obi-Wan Kenobi, Yoda, and his father, Anakin Skywalker.

The Force was with Luke—and would be with him always!